melanie walsh
my nose, your nose

Picture Corgi

Daisy's skin is brown.

Agnes's skin is white. But...

they both have cheeky
Pink tongues!

Arthur's hair is
brown and straight.

Kit's hair is black
and curly. But...

they both hate washday!

Arthur's nose turns up.

Agnes's nose turns down.

But...

they both like the smell

of chocolate cake!

Daisy has short legs.

Kit has long legs. But...

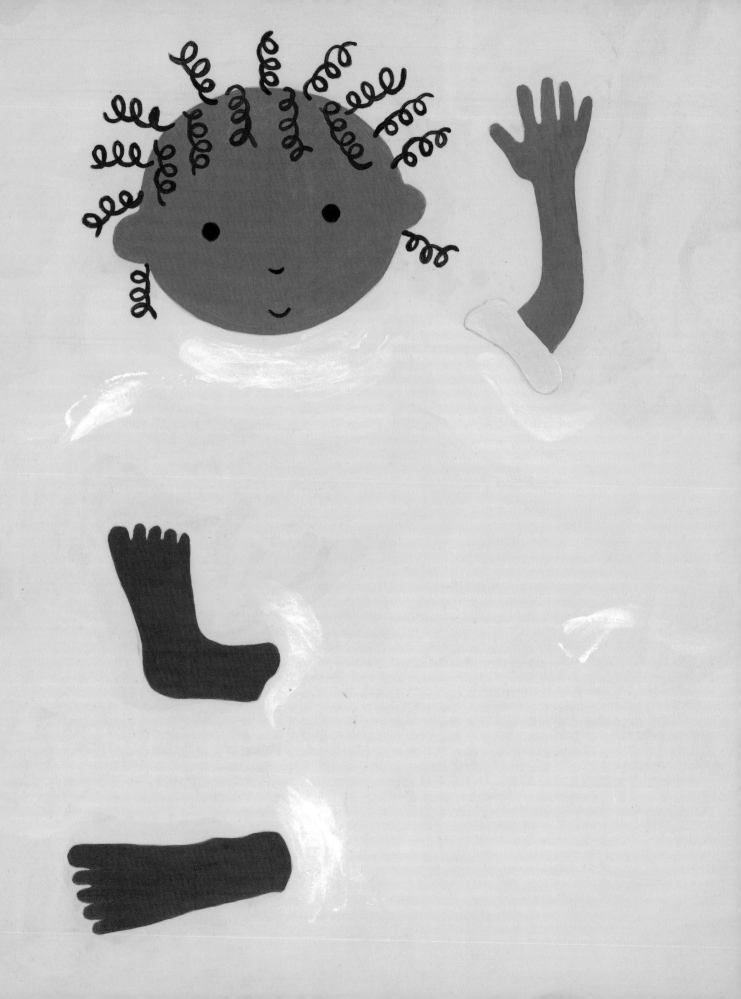

they both kick hard
in the swimming pool!

Agnes has blue eyes.

Kit's eyes are brown.

Arthur has grey eyes.

Daisy's are green. But ...

they all close their eyes

when they go to sleep.

MY NOSE, YOUR NOSE
A PICTURE CORGI BOOK 0 552 547662

First published in Great Britain by Doubleday,
an imprint of Random House Children's Books

Doubleday edition published 2002
Picture Corgi edition published 2003

1 3 5 7 9 10 8 6 4 2

Copyright © Melanie Walsh, 2002

The right of Melanie Walsh to be identified as the author of this work has been
asserted in accordance with the Copyright, Designs and Patents Act 1988.

All rights reserved.

Picture Corgi Books are published by Random House Children's Books,
61–63 Uxbridge Road, London W5 5SA, a division of The Random House Group
Ltd. London, Sydney, Auckland, Johannesburg

THE RANDOM HOUSE GROUP Limited Reg. No. 954009
www.**kids**at**r**andomhouse.co.uk

A CIP catalogue record for this book is available
from the British Library.

Printed in Singapore